Lily Long Pockets

by Clare De Marco

Illustrated by Benedetta Giaufret and Enrica Rusinà

FRANKLIN WATTS
LONDON • SYDNEY

First published in 2015 by
Franklin Watts
338 Euston Road
London
NW1 3BH

Franklin Watts Australia
Level 17/207 Kent Street
Sydney
NSW 2000

A CIP catalogue record for this book is available
from the British Library.

ISBN 978 1 4451 3770 4 (hbk)
ISBN 978 1 4451 3773 5 (pbk)
ISBN 978 1 4451 3772 8 (library ebook)
ISBN 978 1 4451 3769 8 (ebook)

Series Editor: Jackie Hamley
Series Advisor: Catherine Glavina
Series Designer: Peter Scoulding

Printed in China

Franklin Watts is a division of
Hachette Children's Books,
an Hachette UK company.
www.hachette.co.uk

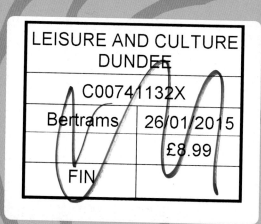

Lily liked to carry treasures.

3

Sometimes it was
bubble mix ...

... a ball

or a toy.

And she always took paper, crayons and stickers.

"You can't carry all that on your scooter," said Dad.

7

"I can – in my pockets," said Lily.

That's just what
Lily did.

Soon, Lily's pockets
got holes in them.

"They're too full,"
said Dad.

14

"I know," said Lily.
She got some
old socks.

Dad helped her to sew the socks into her coat.

"Now I have long pockets!" said Lily.

Puzzle Time!

a

b

c

d

e

That won't fit!

f

Put these pictures in the right
order and tell the story!

sad

happy

fed up

excited

Which words describe Lily when her pockets get holes and which describe her at the end of the story?

Turn over for answers!

Notes for adults

TADPOLES are structured to provide support for newly independent readers. The stories may also be used by adults for sharing with young children.

Starting to read alone can be daunting. **TADPOLES** help by providing visual support and repeating words and phrases. These books will both develop confidence and encourage reading and rereading for pleasure.

If you are reading this book with a child, here are a few suggestions:

1. Make reading fun! Choose a time to read when you and the child are relaxed and have time to share the story.
2. Talk about the story before you start reading. Look at the cover and the blurb. What might the story be about? Why might the child like it?
3. Encourage the child to employ a phonics first approach to tackling new words by sounding the words out.
4. Invite the child to retell the story, using the jumbled picture puzzle as a starting point. Extend vocabulary with the matching words to pictures puzzle.
5. Give praise! Remember that small mistakes need not always be corrected.

Answers

Here is the correct order:
1.d 2.b 3.f 4.a 5.c 6.e

Words to describe Lily when her pockets get holes:
fed up, sad

Words to describe Lily at the end of the story:
excited, happy